MW01131892

Let Freedom Ring

The Battle of Gettysburg:
Turning Point of the Civil War

by Gina DeAngelis

Consultant:
Stephen E. Osman
Historic Fort Snelling, Minnesota

Bridgestone Books
an imprint of Capstone Press
Mankato, Minnesota

Bridgestone Books are published by Capstone Press,
151 Good Counsel Drive, P.O. Box 669, Mankato, Minnesota 56002.
www.capstonepress.com

Printed in the United States of America.

Library of Congress Cataloging-in-Publication Data
DeAngelis, Gina.
The Battle of Gettysburg: Turning Point of the Civil War / by Gina DeAngelis.
    p. cm.—(Let freedom ring)
    Summary: Explains the events leading up to the Battle of Gettysburg and
its importance in the Civil War. Sidebars include information on Union generals and the text
of Abraham Lincoln's Gettysburg Address.
    ISBN 0-7368-1340-3 (hardcover)
    ISBN 0-7368-4516-x (paperback)
1. Gettysburg (Pa.), Battle of, 1863—Juvenile literature. [1. Gettysburg (Pa.), Battle of, 1863.
2. United States—History—Civil War, 1861–1865—Campaigns.] I. Title.
II. Series.
E475.53 .D43 2003
973.7'349—dc21   2001008436

Editorial Credits

Blake A. Hoena, editor; Kia Adams cover and series designer; Juliette Peters, book designer;
Erin Scott, SARIN Creative, illustrator; Kelly Garvin, photo researcher; Karen Risch, product
planning editor

Photo Credits

Bettmann/Corbis, cover; National Park Service, 5; Stock Montage, Inc., 7, 8, 11, 22, 25, 31,
35; Corbis, 12, 16, 41, 42, 43; Visuals Unlimited, 19; Tria Giovan/Corbis, 20; North Wind
Picture Archives, 21, 23, 39 (left); Unicorn Stock Photos, 26; Historic Print & Map Co., 33,
37; Library of Congress, 39 (right); Mark Gibson/Visuals Unlimited, 40

2   3   4   5   6   07   06   05

Table of Contents

Chapter One

A War Between Brothers

People often refer to the Civil War (1861–1865) as a war between brothers. It divided the United States into North and South—the Union and the Confederacy. It also divided families as people chose sides in the war.

Brothers Wesley and William Culp grew up in Gettysburg, Pennsylvania. In 1858, Wesley moved to Virginia with his employer. When the Civil War began, Wesley joined the Confederate Army like many of his friends in Virginia. William also became a soldier, but he still lived in Pennsylvania and it was part of the Union. He joined the Union Army.

In the summer of 1863, the war brought Wesley home to Gettysburg. On his uncle's farm, a place called Culps Hill became the center of one of the war's most important battles. The Battle of Gettysburg helped decide the outcome of the Civil War.

Wesley Culp died during the Confederate's attack of Culps Hill.

Issues of the Civil War

In the early 1800s, the United States' economy was changing. Most Americans still lived on farms, but the North's economy was based on producing and selling factory goods. The North's population grew as European immigrants moved to the United States in search of factory jobs. In the South, the economy was based on agriculture. Southerners grew crops, such as cotton and rice, on large farms called plantations. They depended on slave labor to work these farms. Slavery was unnecessary in the North and many Northern states had outlawed it.

The United States was also expanding during the 1800s. Thousands of Americans were moving west to settle new lands. As territories filled with settlers, new states formed. People in the new states then elected representatives to Congress. These lawmakers voted for issues important to the people in their state.

Lawmakers from Northern and Southern states disagreed on whether slavery should be legal in new states. Slave states and free, or nonslave, states often voted against each other on important issues in Congress. The North did not want any new slave states voting on issues in Congress. The South did not want free states to be able to control Congress.

Northern and Southern leaders also disagreed on how much power the U.S. government should have. Northern leaders believed that there should be a strong central government to make laws for the whole nation. Many Southerners believed it was up to each state to make its own laws. In this way, leaders of new states could decide whether or not to legalize slavery.

Lawmakers in Congress often argued over important issues such as slavery.

The War Begins

Abraham Lincoln was a candidate for president in the 1860 election. He promised not to abolish, or end, slavery where it existed. But Lincoln did not want slavery to spread into new states. Although few Southerners voted for Lincoln, he still won the election.

Many Southerners did not believe Lincoln's promise not to end slavery. In December 1860, South Carolina seceded, or withdrew, from the

The first major battle of the Civil War was called the Battle of Bull Run by Northerners. Southerners called it the Battle of Manassas. The battle ended in a Union defeat.

United States. By February 1861, six more Southern states joined South Carolina in seceding. These seven states formed their own nation called the Confederate States of America, or the Confederacy. Jefferson Davis became their president. Eventually, four more Southern states joined the Confederacy.

At first, Lincoln did not want to go to war with the Confederacy. But he wanted to preserve the Union. The Civil War did not begin until April 1861, when Confederate troops fired on Union soldiers at Fort Sumter near Charleston, South Carolina. Thousands of young men quickly joined the Union and Confederate Armies. They were eager to fight for the side they believed was right. Northern soldiers were called federals. Southern soldiers were called rebels.

The first major battle of the Civil War was fought in July 1861, near Manassas, Virginia. Politicians, reporters, and sightseers followed the Union Army as it marched toward Confederate forces. Many Northerners thought the Union would win the war in just one battle. But Confederate troops defeated the Union Army. After this battle, both sides realized the war would not be over quickly.

Chapter Two

A Bold Plan

At the beginning of the war, the North seemed to have all the advantages. The Union had factories to produce supplies, such as ammunition and uniforms, for its soldiers. The North also had more than twice the population of the South and could form a larger army.

But the Union Army had trouble taking advantage of these strengths. It suffered many early defeats because of poor leadership. In December 1862, the Union Army lost 13,000 men in the Battle of Fredericksburg, Virginia. Many of the soldiers died when General Ambrose Burnside ordered them to attack rebel forces hiding behind a stone wall at the top of a hill. In May 1863, Confederate General Robert E. Lee defeated Union General Joseph Hooker at the Battle of Chancellorsville, Virginia. The Union Army lost this battle even though Hooker's forces were almost double the size

General Lee's troops defeated the Union Army at the Battle of Chancellorsville.

Lincoln's Generals

Poor leadership led to many defeats for the Union Army and often forced Lincoln to change commanders of the army. Initially, he chose Robert E. Lee to command the Union Army. But Lee was from Virginia and he joined the Confederate Army.

General Irwin McDowell commanded the Union Army during its first defeat at Manassas, Virginia. Later, George McClellan led the Union Army. But Lincoln was not pleased with McClellan's command. Lincoln replaced McClellan with General Ambrose Burnside. Shortly after the Battle of Fredericksburg, Virginia, General Joseph Hooker replaced Burnside. General George Meade took over command of the army after the Union's defeat at Chancellorsville, Virginia.

Toward the end of 1863, Lincoln gave command of the Union Army to General Ulysses S. Grant. Grant had captured the important Confederate city of Vicksburg, Mississippi. He led the Union Army for the remainder of the war. In April 1865, Grant forced the Confederate Army's surrender at Appomattox, Virginia.

of Lee's. By mid-1863, the South had won so many victories that some Northerners were beginning to feel that the Union should end the war.

A Daring Plan

Despite Confederate victories, the South was suffering. Virginia suffered the most because it shared its northern border with the Union. Two years of warfare had destroyed Virginia's farmland and economy. Further west in Mississippi, the city of Vicksburg was under siege. Union troops had surrounded the city. Vicksburg was the last Confederate-controlled city on the Mississippi River. If it fell to the Union, the Confederacy would be cut in half. Its western states could not send needed supplies to the eastern states.

In late May 1863, Lee proposed a daring plan to Jefferson Davis. Lee wanted to invade the North. An invasion might draw Union soldiers away from the siege at Vicksburg. It also would give Virginia time to recover. The Confederate Army could take its supplies from Pennsylvania farms.

At best, a Confederate victory in the North could end the war. The Confederate Army could cut off Washington, D.C., from the rest of the Union. If the invasion was successful, Great Britain and France might recognize the Confederacy as an independent nation. The Confederacy needed the support of these countries.

On the other hand, if the Confederate Army lost in the North, it might lose the war. Its army would be in enemy territory. But Lee was confident that his army would not lose.

Invasion of the Union

In June 1863, Lee marched north with 75,000 soldiers. He divided these troops into three groups called corps. One of Lee's trusted generals commanded each corps. These generals were James Longstreet, Richard Ewell, and Ambrose Hill.

Lee's cavalry was commanded by James Ewell Brown "Jeb" Stuart. Stuart's troops rode ahead of Lee's forces to search for the Union Army. Stuart promised to meet Lee in a few days to report the

The Border States

Most slave states joined the Confederacy. But Missouri, Kentucky, Delaware, and Maryland were slaves states that remained in the Union. They were called border states.

Union Army's location. He rode east and then north. He actually rode around the Union Army. In the meantime, Lee moved his army into Pennsylvania.

"Jeb" Stuart commanded Lee's calvary during the events that led up to the Battle of Gettysburg.

General George Meade now commanded the Union Army. He marched his troops between the rebels and Washington, D.C. He wanted to protect the U.S. capital.

As it marched, the Union Army filled roads and river crossings. Stuart could not easily ride around the Union Army to report back to Lee. Meanwhile in Pennsylvania, Lee believed that the Union Army was still far away because he had not heard from Stuart. Lee even thought the Union Army might be in Virginia. He then decided it was safe to spread his army out across the countryside.

This decision allowed Lee's soldiers to search for food and supplies. The Confederates found milk, butter, and other food items that they had not had in war-torn Virginia for some time. Lee ordered his troops to respect the people in the North and their property. But they took government property, such as horses, wagons, and supplies. The Confederates hoped that Pennsylvanians would feel the sting of war as Virginians had.

Chapter Three

The Battle of Gettysburg Begins

When General Lee heard that the Union Army was only about 35 miles (56 kilometers) away, he decided to gather his army quickly. He sent messages to his generals to meet at a nearby town where many roads came together. This town was Gettysburg.

At the same time, General Meade sent out his cavalry to find Lee's troops. Meade wanted to know exactly where the Confederate Army was. He then could plan his defense. Meade wanted to place his troops between Lee's army and Washington, D.C. and wait for Lee to attack.

On July 1, 1863, Meade received a message from one of his cavalry generals, John Buford. Buford had found a large part of Lee's army near Gettysburg.

Robert E. Lee's leadership led to many Confederate victories before the Battle of Gettysburg.

Myth vs. Fact

MYTH: The Battle of Gettysburg began as a fight over shoes when a Confederate leader saw a newspaper advertisement for shoes and wanted to get some for his troops.

FACT: Gettysburg was the easiest place for General Lee to assemble the spread-out pieces of his army. Many roads led into town. For the Union Army, it was important to find the rebels, and they were at Gettysburg.

The First Day of Battle

On July 1, Buford's 2,500 soldiers gathered on a ridge west of Gettysburg. Soon, foot soldiers of the Confederate infantry approached. They had been sent to find out how many Union troops were at Gettysburg. The Battle of Gettysburg started as these two groups met and began to fight.

The Union soldiers held off the rebels for a while. But more Confederate soldiers arrived and pushed Buford's troops back through the streets of town.

Union troops were forced to retreat from the town of Gettysburg during the first day of battle.

Near sunset, the federals gathered on two hills south of town. The hills were called Culps Hill and Cemetery Hill. Union soldiers decided to stay and defend these hills. This plan would force the Confederates to fight uphill. The Union soldiers used rocks, trees, and earth to fortify the hills.

General Lee had not wanted to begin a battle until his army was together. But upon arriving in Gettysburg, he saw that his troops were winning the fight. Lee sent a message to General Ewell to attack Culps Hill and Cemetery Hill, if possible. But Ewell decided to wait until morning.

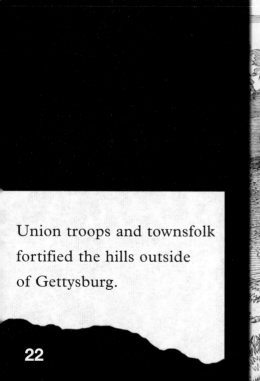

Union troops and townsfolk fortified the hills outside of Gettysburg.

John Burns

John Burns was a Gettysburg resident. He had fought in the War of 1812 (1812–1814) and in the Mexican War (1846–1848). At the time of the Battle of Gettysburg, he was more than 70 years old.

Burns joined a Union regiment marching past his house and

fought in the Battle of Gettysburg. He was the only Gettysburg resident to defend the town.

"He was wounded twice and run over by both armies," Union soldier John Haley recalled, "but [managed] to knock several Confederates off their pins."

Chapter Four

The Second Day of Battle

During the night of July 1, more Union soldiers arrived in Gettysburg. Some joined the men on Culps Hill and Cemetery Hill. Others moved to a high ridge south of Gettysburg called Cemetery Ridge. Cemetery Ridge became lower farther south at a peach orchard and a wheat field. Two hills called Round Top and Little Round Top rose at the end of the ridge.

General Meade arrived that same night. He knew that Lee was a brilliant military leader. He did not want to make any mistakes that could give Lee an advantage. Meade decided it would be best for his troops to defend the hills around Gettysburg rather than attack the rebels.

Throughout the night, more troops arrived on both sides. The Union Army numbered about 85,000 soldiers. Lee's army had about 75,000 soldiers.

Confederate troops attacked Union forces on Cemetery Hill during the second day of the battle.

In His Own Words

Colonel Joshua Chamberlain commanded the 20th Maine. "I saw the faces of my men, one after another, when they had fired their last [bullet], turn anxiously towards mine for a moment, then square to the front again . . . There was nothing for it, but to take the offensive. I stepped to the [flag]. The men turned towards me. One word was enough—'BAYONETS!' —It caught like fire, and swept along the ranks."

Little Round Top

On July 2, at about 4:00 in the afternoon, General Longstreet's troops attacked Union forces near the Round Top hills. The fighting was fierce. In a Union regiment from Minnesota, more than 80 percent of the men were killed or wounded in the first five minutes of fighting. Union General Dan Sickles's leg was shot almost completely off. Sickles lit a cigar as he was carried from the battlefield. He wanted to appear brave so that his troops would not lose hope and would continue to fight.

Union General Gouverneur Warren saw that there were no soldiers on the Round Top hills. Thick woods on Round Top made it too difficult for either army to move troops there quickly. But whichever army put cannons on Little Round Top could easily fire upon the entire battlefield. Four Union regiments arrived on the hills just minutes before Confederate troops attacked.

One regiment, the 20th Maine Volunteers, was on the south end of the Union line, at Little Round Top. Again and again, Confederate soldiers attacked. But the 20th Maine held them back. At last, there were few men left who were able to fight and these soldiers had run out of ammunition. Their leader, Colonel Joshua Chamberlain, ordered his men to attack with bayonets. These metal blades were attached to the ends of their rifles.

The 20th Maine's charge forced the rebels to retreat. This action ended the fighting on Little Round Top. The 20th Maine also captured hundreds of Confederate soldiers.

Culps Hill and Cemetery Hill

At the northern end of the Union line, the rebels attacked Culps Hill and Cemetery Hill around 8:00 at night. Many of the Union troops on Culps Hill had been sent to help on Little Round Top. The soldiers who were left fought hard. They successfully pushed back the Confederate forces.

Some Confederate soldiers from Louisiana reached the top of Cemetery Hill. For a moment it looked as if they might win the battle. But Union troops fought back and pushed the attackers down the hill. Around midnight, the fighting finally stopped.

Lee believed that if neither end of the Union line gave way, then it must be weak in the center. General Longstreet disagreed. He told Lee the Union line was not weak anywhere. He thought the Confederate Army should march around the Union Army and find its own high ground to defend.

"The enemy is there, and I am going to fight him there," Lee told Longstreet. He wanted Longstreet's men to attack the center of the Union line the next day.

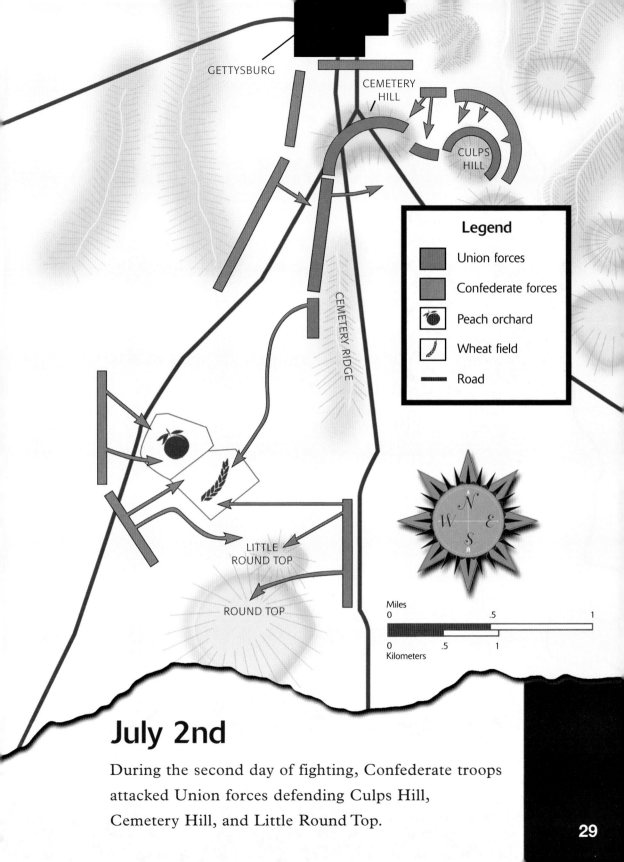

GETTYSBURG

CEMETERY HILL

CULPS HILL

Legend

Union forces

Confederate forces

Peach orchard

Wheat field

Road

CEMETERY RIDGE

LITTLE ROUND TOP

ROUND TOP

Miles
0 .5 1

0 .5 1
Kilometers

July 2nd

During the second day of fighting, Confederate troops attacked Union forces defending Culps Hill, Cemetery Hill, and Little Round Top.

Chapter Five

The High Tide of the Confederacy

Among General Longstreet's commanders was General George Pickett. Pickett commanded 5,000 Virginians. They were considered some of the Confederacy's best soldiers.

At 12:50 on the afternoon of July 3, Confederate cannons began firing at the center of the Union line. Meanwhile, about 13,000 Confederate soldiers, including Pickett's troops, prepared to attack.

Pickett's Charge

At about 2:30, Longstreet ordered Pickett to advance. The distance across the field to the Union line was .75 mile (1.2 kilometers). Pickett ordered his troops to walk quickly and keep close together. They marched toward a clump of trees near the middle of the Union line.

Through the cannon smoke, the federals could see the long lines of Confederate soldiers. Union soldiers watched

Pickett's charge was one of the most important events of the Battle of Gettysburg.

Jennie Wade

Twenty-year-old Jennie Wade hid with her family in her sister's cellar as soon as the fighting started. When Jennie came out to bake bread, a stray bullet went through two wooden doors and hit her in the back. She died instantly. Jennie was the only Gettysburg resident to be killed during the battle.

as the enemy approached. When the rebels slowed to climb a fence, Union soldiers began to fire their own cannons. The Confederate line began to fall apart as hundreds of men were killed or wounded.

High Tide of the Confederacy

Union soldiers waited for the Confederate soldiers behind a low stone wall. The fighting was most fierce where this wall turned a corner, later called "The Angle." Some historians call this point the "High Tide of the Confederacy," because it was the closest the South came to defeating the Union Army and winning the war.

By about 4:00 in the afternoon on July 3, Pickett's charge was finished. More than half of his men were dead or wounded. During the fighting that day, more than 6,000 Confederate troops were wounded, killed, or taken prisoner. The Confederates had suffered a major defeat.

Pickett led his troops up Cemetery Ridge, but he was unable to defeat the Union forces that defended the ridge.

Chapter Six

The Gettysburg Address

Northerners were both overjoyed at the victory yet horrified by the loss of life. Both armies suffered great losses at the Battle of Gettysburg. More than 23,000 Union soldiers were killed, wounded, or captured. The Confederate Army lost 28,000 soldiers. This number was more than one-third of General Lee's army. The Confederacy would continue to fight on, but its army never fully recovered from the Battle of Gettysburg.

It rained during the night of July 3rd, soaking the thousands of men who lay wounded on the fields near Gettysburg. When Lee's army left the next night, those wounded who could not be moved were left behind and captured by the Union Army. Lee's army began to retreat south. Its wagon trains stretched for 17 miles (27 kilometers).

Lee's defeated troops were forced to retreat from Gettysburg.

President Lincoln urged General Meade to follow Lee quickly. But Meade wanted to give his soldiers a rest after the battle.

Lee's army was forced to stop at the Potomac River before reaching Virginia. That stop would have been a perfect time for Meade to attack. But Lee's soldiers quickly built a bridge to cross the river. Lee's army escaped by the time Meade's forces arrived.

Vicksburg Surrenders

On July 4, General John Pemberton surrendered his 31,000 Confederate soldiers to General Ulysses S. Grant at Vicksburg. The Union then controlled the Mississippi River. It could use the river to transport soldiers and supplies. This Confederate defeat also cut off eastern states of the Confederacy from supplies in western states.

Together, the surrender of Vicksburg and the Battle of Gettysburg were a turning point in the war. Before Gettysburg, it did not seem as if the Union could defeat the Confederacy. But the South's army suffered two important losses. The war would drag on for two more bloody years. But after Gettysburg, the Union seemed certain to win.

The Gettysburg Address

On November 19, 1863, a national cemetery was
dedicated at Gettysburg. This memorial honors the
soldiers who fought and died in the Battle of
Gettysburg. Edward Everett, a famous speaker of
the time, gave a speech. President Lincoln also was
asked to address the crowd.

General Grant's forces were unable to defeat Confederate troops at
Vicksburg, but a siege of the city led to a Confederate surrender.

Gettysburg Address — A. Lincoln, 11/19/1863

Four score and seven years ago our fathers brought forth on this continent a new nation conceived in Liberty, and dedicated to the proposition that all men are created equal.

Now we are engaged in a great civil war, testing whether that nation or any nation so conceived and so dedicated, can long endure. We are met on a great battle-field of that war. We have come to dedicate a portion of that field, as a final resting place for those who here gave their lives that that nation might live. It is altogether fitting and proper that we should do this.

But, in a larger sense, we can not dedicate—we can not consecrate—we can not hallow—this ground. The brave men, living and dead, who struggled here have consecrated it, far above our poor power to add or detract. The world will little note, nor long remember what we say here, but it can never forget what they did here. It is for us the living, rather, to be dedicated here to the unfinished work which they who have fought here have thus far so nobly advanced. It is rather for us to be here dedicated to the great task remaining before us—that from these honored dead we take increased devotion to that cause for which they gave the last full measure of devotion—that we here highly resolve that these dead shall not have died in vain—that this nation under God shall have a new birth of freedom—and that government of the people, by the people, for the people, shall not perish from the earth.

Everett spoke for more than two hours. It then was Lincoln's turn. His speech is known as the "Gettysburg Address." It described the importance of the battle and the Civil War in only two minutes. Lincoln's words encouraged his listeners to devote themselves to winning the war for freedom, just as the soldiers who died at Gettysburg had done.

At the time, many newspapers made fun of Lincoln's short speech. But within a few months, people realized how special it was. Even today, the Gettysburg Address is considered one of the finest examples of writing in the English language.

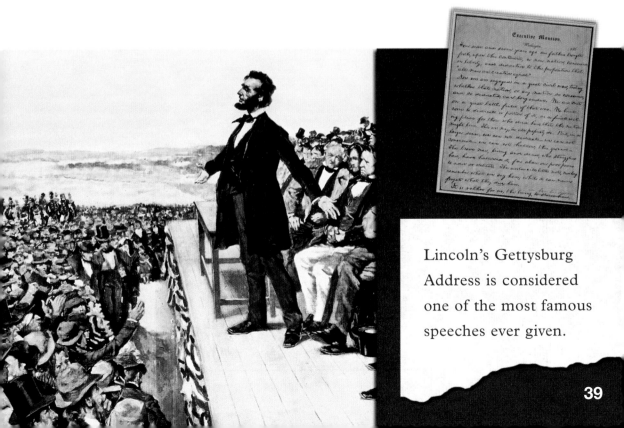

Lincoln's Gettysburg Address is considered one of the most famous speeches ever given.

Gettysburg Today

Today, much of the battlefield near Gettysburg has been preserved as a park. More than 1.5 million people visit this park each year.

Gettysburg National Military Park contains 6,000 acres (2,400 hectares) of land and 23 miles (37 kilometers) of roads. There are more than 1,400 monuments within the park. At the park's visitor center, people can learn more about the battle and the people who fought there. They also can learn about Lincoln and his famous address.

The Civil War, as Lincoln said, tested whether the United States would survive and truly be free. In many ways, Gettysburg was the most important battle of the Civil War. It helped turn the tide of the war and led to the Union's victory.

The North Carolina Monument near Gettysburg honors the soldiers from North Carolina who fought during the Battle of Gettysburg.

TIMELINE

November: Abraham Lincoln is elected president of the United States.

July: The First Battle of Bull Run (Manassas) is fought.

February to June: 10 Southern states join South Carolina to form the Confederate States of America.

December: The Battle of Fredericksburg is fought.

1860   **1861**   **1862**

December: South Carolina secedes from the Union.

April 12: The Civil War begins when Confederate troops fire on Union soldiers at Fort Sumter, South Carolina.

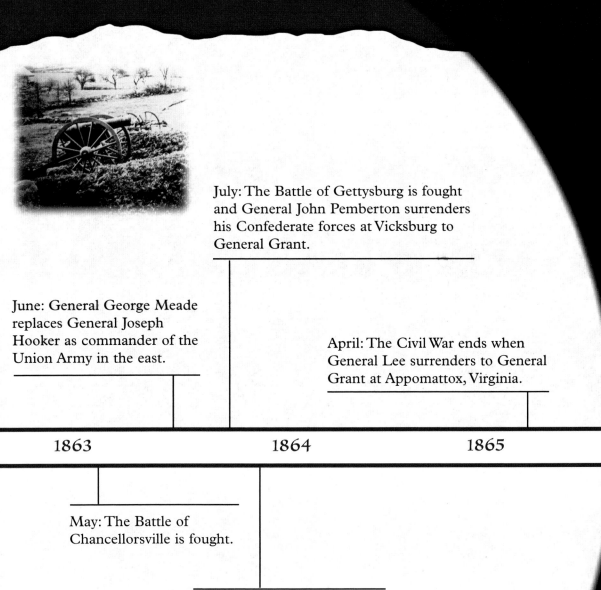

July: The Battle of Gettysburg is fought and General John Pemberton surrenders his Confederate forces at Vicksburg to General Grant.

June: General George Meade replaces General Joseph Hooker as commander of the Union Army in the east.

April: The Civil War ends when General Lee surrenders to General Grant at Appomattox, Virginia.

1863   1864   1865

May: The Battle of Chancellorsville is fought.

November: Lincoln gives his Gettysburg Address at the dedication of Gettysburg National Cemetery.

Glossary

ammunition (am-yuh-NISH-uhn)—objects that can be fired from weapons such as bullets from a rifle

bayonet (BAY-uh-net)—a long metal blade that can be attached to the end of a rifle

cavalry (KAV-uhl-ree)—soldiers who travel and fight on horseback

Confederacy (kuhn-FED-ur-uh-see)—the nation formed by Southern states which seceded from the United States

corps (KOR)—a large part of an army which consists of many different smaller parts, including regiments

federal (FED-ur-uhl)—to be united under one central government; Union Army soldiers were called federals during the Civil War.

fortify (FOR-tuh-fye)—to make a place stronger against attack; Union soldiers fortified the hills around Gettysburg.

infantry (IN-fuhn-tree)—soldiers who travel and fight on foot

plantation (plan-TAY-shuhn)—a large farm found in Southern states on which crops such as rice and cotton are grown

rebel (REB-uhl)—a person who fights against a government; Confederate soldiers were called rebels during the Civil War.

regiment (REJ-uh-muhnt)—a group of up to 1,000 soldiers

secede (si-SEED)—to withdraw from

siege (SEEJ)—the surrounding of a city to cut off supplies and then wait for those inside to surrender

Further Reading

Burgan, Michael. *The Battle of Gettysburg.* We the People. Minneapolis: Compass Point Books, 2001.

Feinberg, Barbara Silberdick. *Abraham Lincoln's Gettysburg Address: Four Score and More.* Brookfield, Conn.: Twenty-First Century Books, 2000.

Gaines, Ann Graham. *The Battle of Gettysburg In American History.* In American History. Berkeley Heights, N.J.: Enslow Publishers, 2001.

Graves, Kerry A. *The Civil War.* America Goes to War. Mankato, Minn.: Capstone Books, 2001.

Monroe, Judy. *Robert E. Lee.* Let Freedom Ring. Mankato, Minn.: Bridgestone Books, 2002.

Stanchak, John. *Civil War.* Eyewitness Books. New York: Dorling Kindersley, 2000.

Places of Interest

Appomattox Court House National Historic Park
Highway 24
P.O. Box 218
Appomattox, VA 24522
http://www.nps.gov/apco
This is the site where Robert E. Lee surrendered to Ulysses S. Grant.

Gettysburg National Military Park
97 Taneytown Road
Gettysburg, PA 17325
The Park provides visitors with information about the Battle of Gettysburg, Lincoln's address, and the Civil War.

General Lee's Headquarters Museum
401 Buford Avenue
Gettysburg, PA 17325
http://www.civilwarheadquarters.com
Visitors can find information on Robert E. Lee, his commanders, and the Southern soldiers who fought at Gettysburg.

Fort Sumter National Monument
1214 Middle Street
Sullivan's Island, SC 29482
http://www.nps.gov/fosu/fosu.htm
This park is at the site of Fort Sumter, where the first fighting of the Civil War began.

Internet Sites

Do you want to learn more about The Battle of Gettysburg?
Visit the FactHound at *www.facthound.com*

FactHound can track down many sites to help you. All the
FactHound sites are hand-selected by our editors. FactHound will
fetch the best, most accurate information to answer your questions.

IT'S EASY! IT'S FUN!
1) Go to *www.facthound.com*
2) Type in: **0736813403**
3) Click on **FETCH IT** and FactHound will put you on the trail
of several helpful links.

You can also search by subject or book title. So, relax
and let our pal FactHound do the research for you!

Index